T0128597

SHELBY AND SHADOW GO SHEEP-HERDING

B.I. PHILLIPS

To order additional copies of this book, contact:
Xlibris
844-714-8691
www.Xlibris.com
Orders@Xlibris.com

ISBN: Softcover   978-1-6698-3885-2
       EBook   978-1-6698-3884-5

Print information available on the last page

Rev. date: 07/19/2022

Grateful acknowledgments: Ketch dog training.

This book belongs to:

_____

Shelby was very excited to realize she had been taken to a sheep herding lesson. I was not quite sure that I understood how it worked. But the expert brought her in with the sheep. There is quite a dance that goes in sheepherding.

Shelby excelled at this. Instantly she picked it up.

Shadow on the other hand was a bit timid. The handler was very gentle and patient.

5

Shadow seemed to be half- heartedly into this activity the first time around. He gave it a good try.

Shadow returned for a second visit. Interesting to note his ears were slightly back and the sheep seemed to move on cue without any or much movement on Shadows part but his presence.

Again he made an attempt. The sheep seemed to know the drill. They were quite beautiful. Well cared for. Shadow did the activity for the allotted safe time for himself and the sheep.

After placing a call to the facility I discovered that this is an actual activity that is considered to be a competition and ribbon worthy.

Later I discovered that some clients motives included bringing their dog there to try out for sheep- herding competition. That was not my objective of course, mainly to provide an activity in which they could use their natural instincts.

13

To this day I'm still not sure what is expected of a dog who competes in sheep- herding.

15

After some research I guess they lose points in a competition if they split the sheep.

Printed in the United States
by Baker & Taylor Publisher Services